ALLEN COUNTY PUBLIC LIBRARY

ACPL ITEM
DISCARDED

STO

D1297231

"WHOO WHOO"

by

CATHRINE BARR

HENRY Z. WALCK, INC.   NEW YORK

1966

Copyright © 1966 by Cathrine Barr. All rights reserved. Library of Congress Catalog Card Number: 66-13950. Printed in the United States of America.

1608483

One night Chuck and Jan looked out the window. They heard a rasping call. A baby owl came from the woods.

He landed shakily on a fence post.
Then another owl followed.

He landed on the next post. And another owl wobbled to a third post.

They made rasping calls, a sign that they were hungry.

Chuck and Jan heard a distant "Whoo-Whoo."

A Great Horned Mother Owl
swished to a nearby tree. She
carried food in her beak.

Quietly she swooped to Owl One and
hung in the air while he took the food.
Silently she left. She returned with food
for Owl Two. And then for Owl Three.

After eating, the baby owls flew
back to their nest in the woods.

The next night Chuck and Jan came to the window again. The baby owls were on the posts, making raspy cries.

Mother Owl called, "Whoo-Whoo."
But she did not bring food. The baby
owls must learn to hunt their own.
"Whoo-Whoo," prompted Mother Owl.

Finally the little owls stopped crying. Owl One watched for movement in the grass. He wobbled, then silently pounced on his dinner and swooped back to the post with it.

Owl Two teetered, then quietly
plunged to the ground and came
back with his meal.

Owl Three watched his brothers.
He watched the ground. He
swayed. He was afraid to dive
down to the ground.

He leaned out, too scared to plunge.
Finally he gave up with a raspy
hungry cry.

"Whoo-Whoo," called Mother Owl, but
she didn't bring him food.

The two full little owls and the
hungry little owl flew back to
the woods.

Again, the following night, Chuck
and Jan watched Owl One and Owl
Two eat. Owl Three was still too
frightened to catch his own dinner.

Then Chuck and Jan had an
idea. The next night, before the
owls came, they put out a piece
of meat tied to a long string.

The string went through the grass
to the window. Inside the house
Chuck held the string in his hand.

They waited. The owls came.

Owl Three could barely wobble to
his post, he was so hungry.

After a few rasping calls, the
hunting began.

Soon One and Two had eaten. They
flew back to the woods. Owl Three
was too hungry to fly.

Chuck and Jan saw him blink at the
ground. Chuck pulled the string.
The meat moved. The owl cocked
his head.

Chuck moved the meat again.

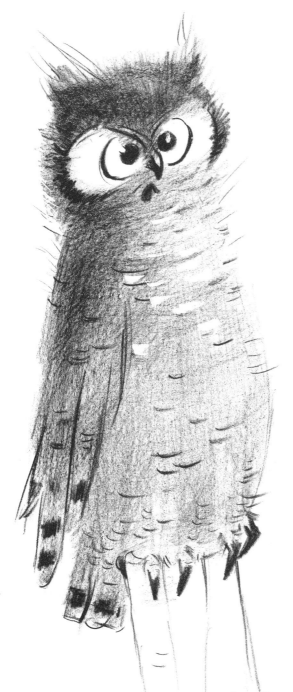

Owl Three leaned forward, then straightened up and looked away in fear.

"Whoo-Whoo," encouraged Chuck,
imitating the Great Horned Owl.
Owl Three swayed. "Whoo-Whoo,"
Chuck called again.

He pulled slowly on the string and
moved the meat steadily along.

Little Owl Three saw the fine dinner
moving away.

"Whoo-Whoo."

Owl Three rocked, then dove to the ground. The meat broke from the string as he went back to his post with it.

He puffed out his chest as
he swallowed his dinner.

1608483

Proudly he flew off to the woods.

"Good boy!" shouted Chuck and Jan.

What happened the next night ?

Chuck and Jan were at the window
to see.

The three little owls came from
the woods together. From the
posts they watched for food.

This time, little Owl Three was the first to swoop smoothly and silently to the ground and back with a fine fat dinner.

"Good boy!" said Chuck as he and Jan smiled.

And from the nearby tree the
Great Horned Mother Owl called,
"Whoo-Whoo."